WHERE'S
ALBERT?

by **Eleanor May** • Illustrated by **Deborah Melmon**

THE KANE PRESS / NEW YORK

Acknowledgments: We wish to thank the following people for their helpful advice and review of the material contained in this book: Susan Longo, Former Early Childhood and Elementary School Teacher, Mamaroneck, NY; and Rebeka Eston Salemi, Kindergarten Teacher, Lincoln School, Lincoln, MA.

Special thanks to Susan Longo for providing the Fun Activities in the back of this book.

Library of Congress Cataloging-in-Publication Data

Names: May, Eleanor, author. | Melmon, Deborah, illustrator.
Title: Where's Albert? / by Eleanor May ; illustrated by Deborah Melmon.
Other titles: Where is Albert?
Description: New York : Kane Press, 2017. | Series: Mouse math | Summary: On a camping trip, the Squeak Scouts practice the math concepts of counting and multiplying, but when Albert gets sidetracked with his pet snail, Flash, the Squeak Scouts must shout, "Where's Albert?"
Identifiers: LCCN 2016019288 (print) | LCCN 2016047810 (ebook) | ISBN 9781575658551 (reinforced library binding : alk. paper) | ISBN 9781575658582 (pbk. : alk. paper) | ISBN 9781575658612 (ebook)
Subjects: | CYAC: Counting—Fiction. | Mice—Fiction. | Camping—Fiction. | Scouting (Youth activity)—Fiction.
Classification: LCC PZ7.M4513 Whe 2017 (print) | LCC PZ7.M4513 (ebook) | DDC [E]—dc23
LC record available at https://lccn.loc.gov/2016019288

1 3 5 7 9 10 8 6 4 2

First published in the United States of America in 2017 by Kane Press, Inc.
Printed in China

Book Design: Edward Miller

Mouse Math is a registered trademark of Kane Press, Inc.

Visit us online at **www.kanepress.com**

 Like us on Facebook
facebook.com/kanepress

 Follow us on Twitter
@KanePress

Dear Parent/Educator,

"I can't do math." Every child (or grownup!) who says these words has at some point along the way felt intimidated by math. For young children who are just being introduced to the subject, we wanted to create a world in which math was not simply numbers on a page, but a part of life—an adventure!

Enter Albert and Wanda, two little mice who live in the walls of a People House. Children will be swept along with this irrepressible duo and their merry band of friends as they tackle mouse-sized problems and dilemmas (and sometimes *cat-sized* problems and dilemmas!).

Each book in the **MOUSE MATH**® series provides a fresh take on a basic math concept. The mice discover solutions as they, for instance, use position words while teaching a pet snail to do tricks or count the alarmingly large number of friends they've invited over on a rainy day—and, lo and behold, they are doing math!

Math educators who specialize in early childhood learning have applied their expertise to make sure each title is as helpful as possible to young children—and to their parents and teachers. Fun activities at the ends of the books and on our website encourage kids to think and talk about math in ways that will make each concept clear and memorable.

As with our award-winning Math Matters® series, our aim is to captivate children's imaginations by drawing them into the story, and so into the math at the heart of each adventure. It is our hope that kids will want to hear and read the **MOUSE MATH** stories again and again and that, as they grow up, they will approach math with enthusiasm and see it as an invaluable tool for navigating the world they live in.

Sincerely,

Joanne Kane

Joanne E. Kane
Publisher

"Okay, Squeak Scouts!" bellowed Agnes, the scout leader. "Time to go on our big campout!"

The Squeak Scouts cheered.

Agnes counted tails to make sure all ten scouts were there.

"**1, 2, 3, 4, 5,**" she counted. "**6, 7, 8, 9** . . .
Wait! I only count nine tails. Where's Albert?"

Albert's sister, Wanda, ran to find him.
"Come on, Albert!" she said. "Everyone is ready."

"I'm waiting for Flash to catch up," Albert explained.

"You're bringing Flash on the campout?" Wanda looked at their pet snail. "Albert, I'm not sure snails like to hike."

"Hmm." Albert frowned. "Maybe you're right."
He took Flash back inside.

"Ta-da!" Albert came back out. "Problem solved! Flash can ride in my red wagon, so he doesn't have to hike."

Wanda and Albert scurried to join the other Squeak Scouts.

Agnes counted tails again.

"**1, 2, 3, 4, 5, 6, 7, 8, 9, 10** mice."

Albert added, "And one snail!"

Agnes led them off into the woods.
"Scamper along, Scouts!" she said.
"We have a long way to go!"

The Squeak Scouts marched uphill . . .

10

. . . and down.

11

After a while they stopped beside a stream.
"I'm hungry enough to eat a chipmunk!" Charlie said.

Agnes smiled. "How about cheesy puffs instead?"

Counting by twos, Agnes gave two cheesy puffs to each of the ten scouts.

"**2, 4, 6, 8, 10, 12, 14, 16, 18** . . ." She stopped. "I still have two left. Where's Albert?"

"Up here!" Albert called, dangling from a bush. "I'm getting Flash a snack. Snails don't eat cheesy puffs, you know."

Albert dropped to the ground.

Handing him the last two cheesy puffs, Agnes counted again.

"**2, 4, 6, 8, 10, 12, 14, 16, 18, 20**.
Two cheesy puffs per scout."

Albert said, "And two delicious leaves for Flash!"

At last the Squeak Scouts reached their campsite.

Agnes showed them how to set up their tents.

"I'll give you tent pegs so your tents don't blow away," she said. "Five pegs for every tent."

Agnes counted by fives as she handed out the pegs.

"5, 10, 15, 20, 25, 30, 35, 40, 45 . . ."

She held up the last five pegs. "Where is Albert *now*?"

Albert poked his head out from a fallen tent.
"I can't make my tent stay up!" he said.

"Albert, where are your tent poles?" Wanda asked.

"Tent poles?" Albert asked. "Uh-oh."

Wanda groaned. "You didn't pack your tent poles?"

"Sure, I packed them!" Albert said. "But the wagon felt so heavy going up that hill, I tossed a few things out. I was going to pick everything back up on the way home."

"We can both squeeze into my tent," Wanda told Albert.
"But Flash will have to sleep outside."

"Flash doesn't need a tent," Albert said.
"He brought his whole house!"

"Time to build the bonfire!" Agnes announced. She told the scouts to go out in the woods and find dry twigs.

"If every scout can carry back ten twigs, we'll have a nice big bonfire." She looked at Albert. "*Every* scout. Okay?"

As the scouts returned with their paws full of twigs, Agnes counted by tens.

"10, 20, 30, 40, 50, 60, 70, 80, 90 . . .
Oh, no. Not again!"

"WHERE'S ALBERT?" all the Squeak Scouts chorused.

"Right here!" Albert called.

Albert dropped his load of twigs. "Here's nine."

"Nine?" Agnes said. "But . . ."

Albert ran back into the woods.

"And here's the tenth!" Albert puffed. "Flash picked it out. Good thing we had the wagon, huh?"

Agnes counted again by tens. This time all the scouts joined in.

"10, 20, 30, 40, 50, 60, 70, 80, 90, *100!*"

As they sat around the fire, Agnes handed out the Squeak Scout songbooks.

"**1, 2, 3, 4, 5**," she counted. "**6, 7, 8, 9 . . .**"

29

"**10!**" Albert finished as he took the last songbook.
"Don't worry—Flash and I can share."

Where's Albert? supports children's understanding of **counting** and **skip counting**, important concepts in early math learning. Use the activities below to extend the math topic and to support children's early reading skills.

🐭 ENGAGE

Remind the children that the cover of a book can tell them a lot about the story inside.

▷ Before reading the story, hold your hand over the title and invite the children to look at the cover illustration. Ask: *What do you think this story is about? Where does it take place? Do you think there is a problem? What could it be?* Listen to all the responses the children provide. Now uncover the title and read it aloud. Did anyone guess that Albert goes missing in this story?

▷ Ask the children if they have ever gone camping. Ask: *What are some important rules you need to know about camping?* Have each child turn to a partner and talk this out. Then have them share their thoughts.

▷ Can the children list supplies they would need to go camping outdoors? Record their responses on a board or on chart paper. Be sure to refer back to this list at the end of the story and fill in any important supplies that are not on the list.

▷ Now read the story to find where Albert's adventures take him when he goes camping with his scout troop!

🐭 LOOK BACK

▷ After reading the story, ask the children to recall parts of the story:
  • Where was Albert when Agnes, the scout leader, counted off the first time, by ones (1–10)?
  • Where was Albert when Agnes counted off the second time, by twos (2–20)?
  • Where was Albert when Agnes counted off the third time, by fives (5–50)?
  • Where was Albert when Agnes counted off the fourth time, by tens (10–100)?

▷ Have each child turn to a partner and discuss the questions below. Have them share their thoughts with the whole group after they're done.
  • Was it safe for Albert to leave the group? Why or why not?
  • If you were in the Squeak Scouts with Albert, what would you have said to Albert or to Agnes when Albert went looking for a yummy snack for Flash?

🐭 TRY THIS!

Count off, count up!

Have the children sit in a circle formation on the rug or in their seats. Explain to the children that they will count off either by ones, twos, fives, or tens. Do a practice run first by having the children count off by ones (see how high they can count with no errors!). If a child misses a number, they must pull back from the circle and the circle will become smaller. The counting continues with the remaining children.

Now re-form the circle and start the count-off again, but this time have children skip count by twos (and then by fives and then by tens). If you wish, you may choose a number, such as 100, where the count will stop and start over from the beginning. The more times children practice this game, the better the chances of having a full circle, complete with all the students, at the end!

🐭 THINK!

Counting made easy!

Provide a bag of 100 buttons or other small, countable objects to a pair of children. Ask the children to count out the buttons in their bag one by one. With a stopwatch, time how long it takes them, and record the time on a sheet of paper.

Next have the children group the buttons into piles of twos. Have them skip count by twos, and record the amount of time it took them. Follow the same steps for piles of fives and tens. Have the children compare the results. Was there a difference in how long it took to count different groupings of the buttons? Why? Ask children whether they think skip counting might be useful when something needs to be counted quickly. What other scenarios can they think of where skip counting may be helpful?

Repeat the activity with the rest of the children until everyone has had at least one turn.

◆ **FOR MORE ACTIVITIES** ◆
visit www.kanepress.com/mouse-math-activities